The Traveler

Eric, Tiffany, & Amber Legge

AuthorHouse™
1663 Liberty Drive
Bloomington, IN 47403
www.authorhouse.com
Phone: 1 (800) 839-8640

Published by AuthorHouse 07/03/2019

ISBN: 978-1-7283-1795-3 (sc)
ISBN: 978-1-7283-1796-0 (hc)
ISBN: 978-1-7283-1797-7 (e)

Library of Congress Control Number: 2019908885

Print information available on the last page.

Any people depicted in stock imagery provided by Getty Images are models,
and such images are being used for illustrative purposes only.
Certain stock imagery © Getty Images.

This book is printed on acid-free paper.

Because of the dynamic nature of the Internet, any web addresses or links contained in this book may have changed
since publication and may no longer be valid. The views expressed in this work are solely those of the author and do
not necessarily reflect the views of the publisher, and the publisher hereby disclaims any responsibility for them.

authorHOUSE®

This book is dedicated

To my two beautiful daughters

Tiffany & Amber

Who helped so much

In the writing of this book.

CHAPTER ONE

Once upon a time, in a land far, far away, lived a Traveler who roamed the countryside. With him he carried only a coat to keep him warm, a blanket to sleep on, a pot to cook his food in, and a bag that he always had tossed over his shoulder. He traveled from village to village, never staying very long, never seen without his bag, and always remembered by all the people in the villages he visited.

One day he wandered into the village of Lost Lakes. The village of Lost Lakes was not a large place and the villagers mostly kept to themselves. When a stranger came into the village, everyone knew that something was out of place. They were not used to stranger in Lost Lakes, and when one did happen to pass through, no one knew what to do or say. Most, simply did not want their peaceful village disturbed.

One of the first to see the Traveler was a little girl named Mary. Mary, like the rest of the villagers, was curious about what the Traveler had in his bag. Everyone asked each other who was this stranger, and what was in his bag?

"Have you ever seen this man before?" the butcher asked the barber.

"No I have not" replied the barber.

"I wonder what he has in that bag of his?" asked the barber.

"I'm not sure, but it might be filled with gold" said the butcher.

"Or maybe there is stolen treasures in there" said the barber.

Everyone in the village was talking about the Traveler, trying to guess what was in the mysterious bag. But the sun had gone down, and the Traveler had made his way to the lake, just outside of town to get ready to go to sleep. He had traveled a long, long, way that day and he was very tired.

Back in the village, the little girl named Mary was also getting ready for bed. As her mother tucked her into bed, Mary asked,

"Mommy, did you see the stranger that came into the village today?"

"Yes I did dear" her mother replied.

"I wonder what he had in the bag he carried over his shoulder." Mary asked with a smile.

"Now don't you get started on what is in his bag, Mary. Everyone in the village is making up wild stories about the stranger and his bag. I don't want you to worry yourself about what the stranger has in his bag. Hopefully he will be gone tomorrow, and the village can get back to normal" said Mary's mother.

"But why do you want the stranger to leave Mommy?" asked Mary, not understanding why her mother was bothered by the new person in their village.

"Because we don't know anything about him, sweetheart."

But he doesn't know anything about us either" said Mary with a puzzled look on her face.

"Well he might be a bad person" her mother said, beginning to get frustrated.

"But he might just be a very nice person, Mommy" exclaimed Mary.

"When you get older you will understand" her mother said "Now please go to sleep."

Mary's mother left her room, shutting the door, leaving her daughter wondering why all the grown-ups were afraid of the stranger. He didn't seem to be someone that Mary was afraid of. She hadn't seen the stranger very closely as he walked through town, but he had smiled at her as he passed by. She had also seen where the Traveler had set up camp down by the lake.

CHAPTER TWO

The next morning, Mary awoke after a night filled with dreams of the Traveler and his mysterious bag. It was a beautiful spring morning, and the air smelled of the honeysuckle that surrounded the village. It was the beginning of a day that seemed to be ready for adventure. A day of mystery that made a little girl helpless to its overwhelming power. Mary was off toward the lake.

As Mary got closer to the lake, she could see smoke in the air and was taken by the wonderful smell of breakfast being cooked over an open fire. It must be the Traveler. Mary followed the sight of the smoke and the smell of what she was certain was bacon and biscuits. Mary had been so excited to find out more about the Traveler, she had run out of the house before her mother had cooked breakfast.

Soon she could see what the smoke was coming from. A small campfire was burning with an old pot, that had obviously been over many campfires in its' days, but the Traveler was nowhere to be found.

Mary did not want to go too close to the campfire for fear the Traveler might return and find her spying on him. And what if the grown-ups were right? What if this traveler was someone to fear?

But Mary was not afraid. Something inside her said that this was not a bad man. He was not going to hurt her. Besides, she simply had to find out what was in that bag. Mary kept a safe distance from the campfire, and pretended to go down to the lake for some water. Still, no sight of the Traveler.

Mary was beginning to get a little frustrated. She was a very stubborn young lady. She had not come this far to simply turn back and go home. More importantly, the bacon was beginning to burn. She worked her way a little closer to the campfire, trying her best not to look too obvious.

"It would be a shame to let that bacon burn" Mary said aloud.

"Would you like some breakfast" came a voice form behind her. Mary was so startled that she almost fell down.

Mary quickly turned around to see where the voice had come from. There stood the Traveler whom everyone in the village was talking about. Up close he seemed much less mysterious than he had from the distance where Mary had first seen him. Now she could see into his eyes. She was certain now that he was not someone to be afraid of.

"No thank you", Mary replied quickly, "I have already eaten this morning, but thank you just the same" she lied, remembering her mother telling her countless times not to accept things from strangers, no matter how hungry you might be.

"Well then how about you sit with me while I eat mine. I do so hate to eat alone" said the Traveler.

Mary again thought of something her mother had said many times. Be polite at the dinner table. This wasn't exactly the dinner table, but it was a good enough excuse for Mary.

"I would be glad to" Mary replied. "And you better take that bacon off the fire or it will burn" Mary added.

The Traveler pulled the bacon off the fire and filled his plate with bacon and biscuits that he had prepared earlier. Poor Mary was starving, and the food did smell so good.

"Are you sure you wouldn't like just a little" the Traveler said, sensing the young girl's hunger.

Mary decided to stick with her story and again replied, "No thank you".

So Mary and the Traveler sat down, and Mary watched him eat the breakfast that she so very much wanted.

"Where do you come from?" Mary asked the Traveler.

"From all over the land" replied the Traveler.

"Don't you have a home?" asked Mary.

"This is my home" answered the Traveler.

"You are from Lost Lakes? Then why do all the villagers call you a stranger?" asked Mary very confused.

"No, no. I have never been to this beautiful village that you call Lost Lakes" replied the Traveler.

"But I thought you said this was your home" asked Mary.

"Wherever I build my fire is my home" said the Traveler.

"Can I ask you something else?" asked Mary, hoping the Traveler would not mind all these questions.

"Certainly" replied the Traveler, "Ask anything you wish".

"What is in that bag of yours?" asked Mary.

"As a matter of fact, I have something in here for you, Mary" said the Traveler.

The Traveler reached into his bag and pulled out something small and round. It looked almost furry and must have felt soft to the touch.

"This is for you" said the Traveler.

"I'm sorry, but my mother said I cannot accept things from strangers" said Mary sadly because she really did want to see what this object was.

"I understand" said the Traveler. "Your mother is right, and you are a fine young lady to listen to her. I'll tell you what, I will leave it here on this tree stump while I go fishing at the lake, and you can ask your mother if it is alright for you to have it".

Mary began to get excited as the Traveler finished his breakfast, and began to walk down to the lake. As he was walking away Mary asked, "What is this thing anyway?"

"It is a Warm Fuzzy, and it is all yours" said the Traveler, and he was gone.

Mary stood there not knowing what to do. The Traveler had called her Mary. She was sure she had not told him what her name was. How did he know her name was Mary?

She wanted to pick the object up and examine it, but she remembered what both her mother and the Traveler had told her. Mary ran home as fast as she could to ask her mother if she could accept the gift from the Traveler.

CHAPTER THREE

As Mary ran home, thoughts of the mysterious Warm Fuzzy kept going through her mind. Was it some kind of ball that you play with? Or maybe it was some kind of animal from a far away land that no one in their village had ever seen. It might even be valuable. What if someone found it and took it before she could get back? This made Mary run even faster.

When Mary reached her house, she threw the door open and yelled

"Mommy, Mommy!" at the top of her lungs. Mary's mother ran into the room afraid that Mary had hurt herself.

"Mommy, Mommy, I met the Traveler and he gave me a present. Can I keep it Mommy, oh please can I keep it?" screamed Mary.

"You didn't go see that stranger, did you?" asked her mother with an angry voice.

"But Mommy, he is a very nice man, and he gave me a present out of his bag. We must hurry Mommy, or someone else will find my Warm Fuzzy" said Mary in a panic.

"Mary, I told you never to take things from strangers" her mother said.

"I didn't, Mommy. The Traveler left it on a tree stump and told me to ask you if it was alright for me to take it".

Mary's mother seemed angry that Mary had gone to see the Traveler, but she too was just as curious about what was in that bag as her daughter. Besides, the Traveler had told her daughter to ask her first if she could accept the gift. But what in the world was a Warm Fuzzy. Now Mary's mother was beginning to wonder what was out there on that tree stump by the lake.

"Alright Mary, we will go out to the tree stump and see what this Warm Fuzzy is".

That was all Mary had to hear. She was out the door running almost before her mother had finished her sentence. Mary's mother had a hard time keeping up with her, but she was getting excited about what a Warm Fuzzy was, too.

When they reached the tree stump, Mary was relieved to find the Warm Fuzzy still there. Mary and her mother just stood there for a while, looking at this strange object. Mary's mother had never seen anything like it either. It was about the size of a small orange with a surface that looked to be very smooth and soft.

"Can I keep it Mommy?" asked Mary.

"I guess so" said her mother, not seeing anything wrong with accepting the Traveler's gift.

Mary reached to pick up the Warm Fuzzy. When she had it in her hand, her eyes lit up, she took a step back, and she cried "Oh Mommy, it is the most wonderful thing I have ever felt!"

Her cry startled her mother.

"What is the matter?" asked her mother.

"It just feels so warm and wonderful" said Mary.

Mary was smiling from ear to ear and there was a look on her face that her mother had never seen before. The look in Mary's eyes made her mother think that this Warm Fuzzy was something very, very special.

"Here Mommy, you must feel this" said Mary, handing the Warm Fuzzy to her mother.

When Mary's mother took the Warm Fuzzy from her, she realized that Mary was not kidding. As soon as she touched the Warm Fuzzy, she felt all warm and happy inside. This was a feeling that was hard to describe because it was like nothing they had ever felt before. It was a feeling that made you think there are no bad things, only good, and you could not stop smiling.

"Isn't that the most wonderful thing in the world" said Mary to her mother.

"Yes, dear, you are right. It is the most wonderful feeling I have ever had" said Mary's mother.

As Mary and her mother walked back to the village, they could not stop smiling and wondered why they felt so good. When they got to the village, all the villagers noticed there was something different about Mary and her mother. There was a glow on their faces that everyone could not help but notice.

"Why Mary," asked the butcher, "what puts such a glowing smile on you and your mother's face?"

"The Traveler gave me a Warm Fuzzy from his bag and it makes you feel wonderful" replied Mary.

Mary then gave the Warm Fuzzy to the butcher, and he too, felt all warm and happy inside. Soon it was all over the village about the Warm Fuzzy and how wonderful it was. Everyone wanted to see it.

CHAPTER FOUR

The next day, the Traveler came into the village. As always, he had his bag with him. As he walked down the street, everyone stared at the Traveler and his bag. A very old woman with a cane was walking down the same street. She walked slowly, and her face looked as though every step was painful to her. As the Traveler approached her, he reached into his bag and handed her a Warm Fuzzy.

The old woman's face turned from pain to joy. Instead of being hunched over, she stood up straight and had a beautiful smile of her face.

"Thank you very much" said the old woman, not really knowing what to say for such a gift.

"You're welcome" said the Traveler "I hope it makes you feel better".

The Traveler continued down the street and went into the butcher's shop.

"Do you have any bacon this morning?" asked the Traveler. "I love bacon in the morning".

"I think I have something here for you" said the butcher.

The butcher pulled out some bacon and said to the Traveler "I saw the Warm Fuzzy that you have little Mary. Do you have any more of them?" asked the butcher.

"Yes I do" replied the Traveler.

"I would like to buy one from you. I will give you the bacon in exchange for the Warm Fuzzy" said the butcher.

"I am sorry" said the Traveler "But it doesn't work that way. A Warm Fuzzy cannot be bought".

The Traveler paid for the bacon, and before he left the butcher's shop, he reached into his bag and gave the butcher a Warm Fuzzy.

One by one, all the villagers either ran into the Traveler or went out to the Lake where he set up camp. Everyone who met the Traveler ended up with a Warm Fuzzy.

News of the Warm Fuzzies reached the King who ruled over Lost Lake. His castle was on top of the mountain that overlooked the village. When he heard of all the excitement of the Warm Fuzzies, he had to get his hands on these things that everyone in the village was talking about. He called on his two best soldiers.

"I have heard that a stranger has come to our village and he carries with him something of great value. I must have these Warm Fuzzies for myself" said the kind. "You two must take this chest of gold and buy this magical bag of Warm Fuzzies from the stranger" the King told his two soldiers.

The soldiers made their way down the mountain and into the village in search of the Traveler. They did not have to ask many people where the Traveler was. Everyone knew where his camp was down by the lake.

When the two soldiers reached the Traveler's camp, the Traveler was sitting on the tree stump where he had left Mary's Warm Fuzzy. He was reading a book given to him by one of the villagers for his kindness.

"Are you the stranger with the magical bag of Warm Fuzzies?" asked one of the soldiers.

"Well, I do not feel like a stranger, but I think I am the man you are looking for" said the Traveler.

"The King wished to give this chest of gold for your bag of Warm Fuzzies" said the soldier.

"I'm sorry" said the Traveler "it does not work that way. You can not buy a Warm Fuzzy. It is only something that can be given away. Here, please give this to the King and tell him I hope he enjoys it" said the Traveler as he reached into his bag for a Warm Fuzzy for the King.

"But the King sent us for the whole bag," said the soldier, "he will not be happy with us if we only bring him one".

"You must understand" said the Traveler, "Warm Fuzzies are things that one person gives to another only because he wants that person to feel good. He cannot give it expecting something in return".

The Traveler then reached into his bag and gave each of the soldiers a Warm Fuzzy. The soldiers were trained not to smile, but they could not help themselves. They both smiled and giggled like little boys.

"Thank you very much" both soldiers said at the same time.

They left the Traveler with their Warm Fuzzies, the chest of gold, and two great big smiles. They made their way back to the castle to bring the news to the King.

CHAPTER FIVE

"What do you mean you don't have the bag of Warm Fuzzies?" screamed the King at the two soldiers. "I sent you there to bring me back the whole bag, not just one".

The soldiers were too frightened to answer the King, but because they still had the Warm Fuzzies in their hands, they were both still smiling.

"WHY ARE YOU TWO SMILING?" screamed the King even louder.

"We are sorry your Highness" said one of the soldiers. "These Warm Fuzzies are very powerful. They make you smile whether you want to or not". The soldier then handed the King his Warm Fuzzy.

The King's angry face turned into the happy face of a boy that just got a pony for his birthday. He laughed, and danced around the castle with the Warm Fuzzy held tightly in his hands. "What a wonderful thing this Warm Fuzzy is" said the King.

The King danced and played for hours in the castle. All the servants were amazed at the King acting this way. He had always acted so serious. Now he was acting like a three year old.

Several hours after the King had put the Warm Fuzzy down, he began to think again how much he wanted all of these Warm Fuzzies. He just had to have them all. They must be so very valuable, thought the King. People would come from all over the world to buy these Warm Fuzzies from the King of Lost Lakes. Other Kings would wish they were him. He then took his Warm Fuzzy and locked it in the castle's safe so no one would get it.

The King called the two soldiers again. "I want you to go back and get the bag of Warm Fuzzies from the stranger. He is giving them away to everyone in the village. If we do not get them soon, he will have given them all away. This time you will bring them back to me, or it's off with your heads. Do you understand?" said the King.

"But the Traveler told us that Warm Fuzzies cannot be sold" said one of the soldiers.

"If he doesn't take the chest of gold for the Warm Fuzzies, then lock him in the dungeon and take the bag from him" yelled the King.

The two soldiers ran from the castle for fear of losing their heads. They made their way back down the mountain to find the Traveler again. When they reached the Traveler's camp, he was again on the tree stump, but this time he looked as though he was expecting the soldiers.

"The King has sent us for the bag of Warm Fuzzies" said one of the soldiers to the Traveler. "Please sell them to us so that we can bring them back to the King and keep our heads".

"I am terribly sorry," said the Traveler, "but they would not be Warm Fuzzies if you were to buy them".

"Then what would they become?" asked the soldier.

"You don't want to know" answered the Traveler.

"We are sorry, but if you don't sell the bag, we will have to throw you in the dungeon and take the bag away" said the soldier.

The Traveler tried and tried to explain to the two soldiers that what they wanted was not possible. But the soldiers were so afraid of losing their heads, they took the bag from the Traveler and threw him in the dungeon.

CHAPTER SIX

When all of the villagers heard that the Traveler had been thrown in the dungeon, they were sad for the Traveler. Then, when they realized that the Traveler would not be able to give out anymore Warm Fuzzies, the villagers hid their Warm Fuzzies where no one could find them.

Meanwhile, the two soldiers brought the Traveler's bag to the King.

"At last I have the magical bag" said the King. "I will be the richest King in all the world".

The King then reached into the bag to pull out a Warm Fuzzy. When he pulled it out, he did not have a smile on his face. The King moaned

"What is this awful, cold thing".

He had not pulled out a Warm Fuzzy, but instead it was a Cold Prickly. It made him feel cold and terrible. He felt unwanted and alone. It was the worst feeling that the King had ever felt.

"What have you brought me?" said the King almost in years.

"I don't understand" said one of the soldiers. "We took the only bag that the stranger had".

"He has tricked us" said the King. "He must have known you were coming, hid the Warm Fuzzies, and put these horrible things in their place".

"Go to the dungeon and bring me the stranger" screamed the King.

The two soldiers ran to the dungeon as fast as they could.

"Where did you hide the Warm Fuzzies" shouted the soldiers, frightened that they might end up in the dungeon. Maybe without their heads!

"I told you they must be given to someone. You cannot steal them, or they will turn into Cold Pricklies," the Traveler said.

"The King wants to talk to you right away." said one of the soldiers. "And if I were you, I'd tell him where you hid the Warm Fuzzies!"

The soldiers took the Traveler to the King.

The King was pacing back and forth with a very unhappy look on his face.

"What have you done with the Warm Fuzzies?" said the King, still very angry.

"I have told your two friends that if you try to buy or steal Warm Fuzzies, they will turn to Cold Pricklies" said the Traveler to the King.

This was not the answer that the King wanted to hear.

"Throw him in the dungeon. We will chop off his heard in a week if he does not tell us where the Warm Fuzzies are" ordered the King.

The soldiers took the Traveler down to the dungeon and locked him up.

"I am sorry we have to do this to you" said one of the soldiers.

"Yes, I am sorry, too" said the other soldier. "You were so nice to us. If you would just tell the King where the Warm Fuzzies are, we could let you go. We might even get him to give you that chest of gold."

"I am afraid you just don't understand what a Warm Fuzzy is" said the Traveler.

CHAPTER SEVEN

Everyone in the village had heard the terrible news of the Traveler being locked in the dungeon, and that the King was going to have his head chopped off in a week if he did not give him the Warm Fuzzies. They all worried more about themselves that the Traveler, for each had gone to where they had hid their Warm Fuzzies, only to find that they had turned into Cold Pricklies. They all wanted their Warm Fuzzies back. No one thought of the poor Traveler in the dungeon. No one except, little Mary.

Mary did want her Warm Fuzzy back, but she was more concerned with the Traveler's head being chopped off. He had been so nice to her and everyone in the village. He gave such a wonderful gift, and never asked anyone for anything in return. Well, Mary was going to help the Traveler get out of the dungeon!

That night, after Mary's mother had tucked her into bed, Mary pretended to fall fast asleep. When she was certain her mother would not come in and check on her, Mary slipped out her window and headed for the castle.

It was very dark that night. The moon hid behind the clouds, and the wind whistled through the trees making scary sounds. Mary was very frightened, but she was determined to help the Traveler.

When she reached the castle, Mary saw two guards protecting the gates that led into the castle. Because it was dark, and because she was so small, she was able to sneak past the guards without them noticing her. She made her way down the dark stairways that led to the dungeon.

At the bottom of the stairs was a large door with a small window covered by bars. The window was too high for Mary to see through, so she found a chair and drug it in front of the door. Little Mary climbed up on the chair and peeked into the window. There on a small bed lay the Traveler.

"Are you awake?" whispered Mary to the Traveler.

"Is that my little friend Mary?" asked the Traveler.

"Yes it is" said Mary, "and I have come to rescue you."

"Why that is very nice of you" said the Traveler, "but these bars are a bit too strong for even someone as determined as you, Mary."

Mary looked at the bars and realized that the Traveler was right.

"But I want to help you" said Mary.

"You have helped me just by coming to see me. It is very nice to know someone cares. Thank you for coming. But it is very late and your mother would be very upset if she knew you were here. You must go back home and not worry about me" said the Traveler.

"I will not go until I figure out how I can help you" said Mary in her stubborn voice. "If I could just find the Warm Fuzzies, I could convince the King to let you go. But before I gave them to him, I would have to give one to the old woman in the village who walks with a cane. My mother said she could not remember the last time she saw the old lady smile the way she did after you gave her a Warm Fuzzy. I you could just tell me where you have hidden them, I could get you out."

"I have not hidden them Mary" replied the Traveler. "You still have them."

"No we don't!" exclaimed Mary. "They have turned all cold and sad."

"They are still Warm Fuzzies" said the Traveler. "It's just that everyone has hidden them and tried to keep them for themselves. When you become selfish, they become Cold Pricklies. If you stop being selfish, and give them to someone you want to feel good, they will become Warm Fuzzies again."

The sound of footsteps suddenly filled the dungeon.

"The guards must be coming down to check on me" whispered the Traveler. "You must run home to your mother. Don't worry about me, I'll be fine, and thanks again for coming."

Mary hid in the shadows of the dungeon, snuck by the guards as they checked on the Traveler, and ran up the stairs that led out of the castle. She ran through the darkness of the night all the way home. Luckily her mother was sound asleep, and did not know about Mary's adventure to see the Traveler.

Mary climbed into her nice safe bed and thought of the things that the Traveler had said. She drifted off to sleep, having dreams of Warm Fuzzies and nightmares of a Traveler with no head.

CHAPTER EIGHT

When Mary awoke the next morning, she laid in bed thinking about what the Traveler had said.

"If you stop being selfish and give them to someone you want to make feel good, they will become Warm Fuzzies" Mary said, repeating what the Traveler had said the night before.

Mary thought for a while. She wanted to make the old woman in the village smile again, but she did not understand how she could. She went to her closet where she had hidden her Warm Fuzzy. When she took it in her hands, it felt as cold as it had before. She could not give something that felt this awful to someone she wanted to make feel good.

Even though Mary was not sure what she was doing, she trusted the Traveler. She took the Cold Prickly into the village in search of the old woman with the cane.

It did not take long to find the old woman because everyone was gathered around the butcher's shop talking about the beheading of the Traveler that was to happen the very next day. Mary made her way through the crowd and approached the old woman.

"This is for you" said Mary in a shy voice.

"What is this" said the old woman. "Does it feel like a Warm Fuzzy?" she asked.

"No, it feels very cold right now, but the Traveler said that if I stop being selfish and think of others, it will turn back into a Warm Fuzzy" said Mary.

"I already have one of those Cold Prickies young lady. When I touched it this morning, it nearly sent me to my grave. Now take that horrible thing away from me" the old woman snapped.

"I just wanted to make you smile again" said Mary with tears in her eyes. Mary turned and started to walk away.

The old woman was very grouchy, but she had a good heart. Seeing the tears in little Mary's eyes made her feel bad. After all, she was just trying to do something nice for her.

"Wait just a moment young lady" said the old woman. "You have come all this way to give me something; it would be impolite not to accept your gift. Besides, my mother always told me it was the thought that counts."

The old woman then extended her hands out for the gift with a sour look on her face, waiting for the cold, sad feeling from the Cold Prickly. When Mary put the Cold Prickly in the old woman's hands, her expression changed immediately. A glowing smile came over her face. The villagers could not understand what was going on.

"What is it?" said the barber, "doesn't it feel all cold and pickly."

"No" said the old woman, "it's a Warm Fuzzy again."

The villagers could not believe what they were hearing. Could it be that this girl had solved the mystery of the Cold Prickly?

The barber turned to Mar and said "How did you do that?"

"It's simple" said Mary, now smiling again, "You just have to take your Cold Prickly, and give it to someone that you want to make happy. But you must not do it for selfish reasons. If you do it for something in return, it will remain a Cold Prickly."

The villagers could not believe it was that simple, but one by one the villagers gave their Cold Pricklies to someone they cared about, and they began to turn back into Warm Fuzzies. There was more happiness in the Village of Lost Lakes than anyone had ever seen.

CHAPTER NINE

The King, however, was still very unhappy. He had heard about all the new Warm Fuzzies in the village. He was certain that this was some kind of trick.

It was the day that the Traveler was to have his head chopped off. The King held in his hand the bag that once had all the Warm Fuzzies. It was now filled with the unwanted Cold Pricklies. This made the King very sad because he remembered how wonderful the Warm Fuzzy had made him feel. The more the King thought about the Cold Pricklies, the more the sadness turned to anger.

"Bring me the stranger at once" screamed the King to his soldiers.

The Traveler was brought to the King.

"Why must you insist on being so stubborn" said the King to the Traveler. "If you had just told me where the Warm Fuzzies were instead of the villagers, I would not have to chop off your head today."

"But your Highness, I have told you where the Warm Fuzzies are. You have them right there in the bag that you have in your hand" said the Traveler. This made the King angry again.

"These do not feel like Warm Fuzzies. They are cold and prickly" said the King.

"That's because you are being selfish and keeping them to yourself" explained the Traveler. "If you give them back to me and let me go, they will turn back into Warm Fuzzies."

The King thought about this for a while and came up with an idea. He gave the bag back to the Traveler and said "Here they are. Now may I have a Warm Fuzzy?"

The Traveler reached into his bag and handed one of the Warm Fuzzies to the King. The King's face did not turn to a smile, but instead into the saddest face anyone had ever seen. He dropped the Cold Prickly to the ground and cried to the Traveler "Why do you treat me like a fool. It is still a Cold Prickly."

"You were not going to let me go, were you? That is why they are still Cold Pricklies. In your heart, you knew that you were lying. You were going to keep the Warm Fuzzies for yourself after they changed back. Warm Fuzzies are not something that you can own. They are a gift from the heart that must be shared with others in order for them to stay alive" said the Traveler to the King.

The King was surprised that the Traveler knew what he had planned. He did know in his heart that he was not going to let the Traveler go. The King looked at the Traveler, and realized that he was not trying to trick him. The King realized that it was his own heart that made them Cold Pricklies, not something that the Traveler was doing to hurt him.

"I am sorry" said the King, "I have not been very nice to you when all you have been to me is kind. Please forgive me. You are free to go, with your bag of Warm Fuzzies."

The Traveler reached down to the floor and picked up the Cold Prickly that the King had dropped to the floor and handed it back to him. The King took it, and the smile came back to his face. He felt all warm and wonderful inside again.

The Traveler started to leave, then turned to see the King dancing about the room again like a little oy and said " Just remember this, give your Warm Fuzzies to others and they will give Warm Fuzzies to you."

The Traveler left the village of Lost Lakes, leaving behind many people with smiles that they had somehow forgotten. He still travels all over the land, passing out Warm Fuzzies to all he meets. Somehow he never seems to run out.

THE END

Printed in the United States
By Bookmasters